Victorious 1

Bryce Walton

Alpha Editions

This edition published in 2024

ISBN : 9789362927507

Design and Setting By
Alpha Editions
www.alphaedis.com
Email - info@alphaedis.com

As per information held with us this book is in Public Domain.
This book is a reproduction of an important historical work. Alpha Editions uses the best technology to reproduce historical work in the same manner it was first published to preserve its original nature. Any marks or number seen are left intentionally to preserve its true form.

VICTORIOUS FAILURE

By BRYCE WALTON

With good reason, Professor H. Klauson hesitated; his wife's arms were holding him with a strangely insistent urgency and fear. He tried to disengage himself, but not with much enthusiasm. Although he had not admitted it to anyone but the Presidium's psycho-medic staff, he was afraid, too. Desperately and helplessly afraid.

"Howard, please." Her pale blue eyes were wide, staring into his with that intimacy only someone loved completely and without compromise ever sees. "Don't go back to the Laboratories, Howard. Don't ever go back again."

He smiled, unsuccessfully. He had never been able to hide anything from Lin.

"But, dear, this is ridiculous. We're scientists! We're not frightened by vague, intangible fears."

Her hands tightened on his shoulders. "We're scientists; so let us admit the obvious. Something doesn't want you to ever complete your research, Howard. We've worked together for ten years, and now you're right on the verge of discovering the secret of life itself. And it means more to humanity than anything else in the history of mankind. But I'm afraid, Howard, and so are you. Whatever is against us stopped you before. Your mind almost broke. It will try again, and this time your mind may not recover."

He managed to push her from him, and immediately he felt lonelier, isolated. His faint laugh sounded foolishly insincere.

"Lin, for the love of science! You sound like a mystic. Any mind is liable to become unintegrated. You talk about invisible, intangible forces. These things can only be in men's minds, dear. No mentality is immune to disorientation."

She sobbed, her head swung back and forth hopelessly. A cloud of lovely hair glinted liquidly in the shifting light from the harmonics glowing from the transparent walls of their apartment. He couldn't leave her in this state.

"Lin, darling, listen to me. I can't abandon my life's work. Particularly something so profoundly important to humanity. One more projection, and my 'closed system' principle will be concluded. After that, think of it, Lin! This is really the one thing mankind has been seeking. All his other activities are only bypaths. With eternal life possible, mankind will have a real reason for struggling onward. Lin—"

"No, Howard," she was saying, brokenly. "There isn't an argument. To me, your mind is more important. Why did your mind black out just before you could finish your last experiment? Why, the whole magnificent psycho-medical staff at the Presidium couldn't find a reason. All the charts show you to be amazingly normal. There is something bigger than our science, Howard. It doesn't intend for you to ever finish your research."

"A woman's intuition?" he said sardonically.

"Not a woman's," she corrected. "Ours. Because you feel it the same as I do."

A sick, vague fear came over him as he stood there nervously, remembering the gleaming, arched height of the biochemistry wards at World Science Presidium. That singularly awful instant just before he could finish his last experiment, when all his mental faculties had crumbled. The microfilm protector had just commenced whirring. Then that final spiraling downward into desperate gray fear and unconsciousness.

There had to be a logical explanation so that whatever blockage stood between him and the conclusion of his research could be torn down. The secret of the single cell had long been his. Whatever that three-dim microphoto film revealed, he and only he could turn the key to open the ultimate secret door into victorious eternity for all mankind. Now he blinked burning eyes. Lin was, of course, right. He felt it, too. A hidden, omnipresent kind of force that would prevent him from completing his research. But such a thought was adult infantilism, at best. A hidden force! In his world there had to be logical sequence of cause and effect. But even the psycho-medic staff hadn't been able to find one.

"Howard," she was saying, lips quivering. "Remember our Moon House?"

Klauson bristled, froze. "I remember. The World gave us a magnificent marble house on the Moon overlooking Schroeter's Canyon—a return favor for my many gifts to mankind. What a juvenile farce. Imagine me sitting up there on the Moon, with you—two futile little escapists, haunted by our own uselessness, and our fears. No, Lin. I've my particular destiny to fulfill. It isn't hiding away on the Moon. I'll never accept retirement on the Moon, or any place else. Either now, or after my research on the life force. I'd rather die than stop working in science."

He started for the exit panel. Her voice cut deeply, slowed him, turned him.

"You're going to the Laboratories again then," she asked faintly, "in spite of what happened before?"

He nodded, but when he tried to say yes, his throat was dry and sticky.

"Good-by, Howard," she said.

She was crying when he left. It made him feel terribly lost and guilty to leave her crying. But he had to. What made it so bad was that Lin had never cried before; she was so strong, emotionally. Without any real cause, this made him more nervous and irritable. But he was one of the world's greatest scientists. Everything must have a cause, somewhere. Sometime.

His gyrocar dropped down on the spacious roof-landing of the Biochemistry Building at the World Science Presidium. It was beginning to rain—solid, heavy, sharp-driving drops that spattered on the dull, plastic mesh as he walked hurriedly across it to the ingress.

"Hello, Professor Klauson. This is a surprise. I didn't know you would be coming back so soon."

Klauson started violently, clutched at his heart. A sudden, shooting pain was there. Yet the staff had found nothing wrong with his mental or physical integration. They had checked and rechecked.

"Oh—it's you—Larry!" He paused, relieved. "You—you startled me, Larry. I didn't see anyone on the landing."

"I just came over to do a little work on my own," Larry explained.

He was a young, enthusiastic, highly capable student biochemist, with a shock of unruly black hair. He had graduated from World Tech seven years ago, and had been Klauson's assistant for five, working with him faithfully, sometimes during those grueling sixty-four hour stretches. He had been the only one with Klauson when he had lost consciousness.

"Didn't expect you back so soon, Professor," said Larry, talking casually as their elevator dropped them down below the sub-floor level into the spacious, almost vaulted silence of Klauson's private laboratories. "Say, Professor, you intend to try to finish up again tonight?"

Klauson stiffened. He was here, he felt capable enough. It was only a matter of a few hours. Why not? Even as a therapeutic measure.

"I believe I will, Larry. I wasn't intending to, but now that you're here, too, I might as well."

Larry said nothing. He stood in the soft, yet full brilliance of the invisible fluoresce, his black, almost blue hair hanging over his eyes. He smiled. Klauson started, he had never quite responded this way to Larry's expression before. It seemed—peculiar, rather strange. He discarded that chain of thought and looked about his laboratory.

Nothing had changed. Not that Klauson had expected things to be different. The microphoto film cabinets stood tier upon tier, a long stretch of recorded effort, a complete step-by-step, intricate process of creating life from that awesome moment when he had known the successful preparation of the first simple colloid and had started on his first organic synthesis.

Through the actual combination of the first molecules and the organic colloid and then the first tiny speck of synthesized protoplasm. The frenzied day and night battle against time. Time, that was the predominant factor in nature that did the trick. But he had compressed millions of years into twenty-five. From simple, organic compound through the simple colloid, the protein, the primitive protoplasm, the simplest unicellular organism, the flagellate and—then the great jump into the structure of the gene, the ferreting-out of that intricate, vital combination that gave man life and maintained it. He had conquered—almost.

The high, arched ceiling in the lab with its glowing columns and its streamlined equipment had been provided him by the entire earth—provided him by man's cooperative faith in himself. Men who would find so much greater an impetus to fight ahead if they only knew that whatever other success they might have, their ultimate end was inevitably life, instead of death.

But he would affirm a greater investment of their faith than their wildest dreams had ever granted him. No other man, or combination of men, in the world could synthesize all the knowledge in those cabinets and emerge with the final answer that he alone could evolve. No one but himself. Larry Verrill might possibly develop some capacity to work on the chain. But unlikely. High specialization had made it Klauson's responsibility alone.

Enthusiasm, eagerness was returning; the fear was gone.

"It's so simple, really, now that it's practically over," he said as he unzipped his aerogel cloak, and stepped toward the microphoto film projector. He was talking mostly to himself, a habit of his, only partly to Verrill.

"Yes," said Larry softly. "I suppose you might call it simple."

"Carrel saw to it that cells with which he experimented had a chance to achieve immortality. Under controlled conditions, the growth proceeds forever, logically. The body, a collection of cells, is a 'closed system.' Like a gyrocar, that's what we called it, didn't we, Larry? No closed system can endure unless it can inspect itself, oil itself, and keep itself in repair. A gyrocar can't do that, but the body can and does, though imperfectly."

Klauson warmed to his subject, and his voice assumed a fresh vigor.

"We've conquered that imperfection! Yet I can hardly believe it myself. People can go on living without that final terrible, unconscious fear of death that must defeat them. One more projection, Larry. One remaining link for correlation. The answer is right here in this projector. An actual three-dimensional record of the very first spark in the heart of the cell itself, the primary bursting of a carbon atom commingling with a single cell, creating life. It's the first and the final record, Larry."

Larry nodded, but his lips were twisted in a rather sad, cynical smile, it seemed to Klauson.

"So simple, isn't it, Professor?"

"Yes, it really is," asserted Klauson, his enthusiasm blinding him to the peculiar reaction of Larry Verrill. "Whatever is revealed in this three-dim projection will contain the final step for the infinite prolongation of human life. When I synthesize it with Compton's H-9 film, we'll have it. Incredible, isn't it?"

"You may not realize just how incredible. How could you?" said Verrill. "Nor I either, for that matter."

Klauson hesitated, his hand frozen above the button that would throw the projector into life. Then, shrugging, his hand started to move down. But it didn't.

For then, unbelievably, terrifyingly, it happened a second time. Professor H. Klauson felt a blackness encompassing the mighty, vaulted laboratory. It closed in tightly, smothering, icy. It wrapped his entire swirling mind in darkness....

A little round man smiled broadly at him from a stool close to his bed in the psycho-ward.

"Remember me, Professor?" His face beamed with self-possession.

"You're the clinic psychologist who handled the other electroencephal checkup," said Klauson quickly. "Or are you?"

"Good recall," commented the psychologist. "Name's Dunnel. I've rechecked your whole file since your—ah—second disorientation. Weak alphas of course; but that's necessary in your type. No disrhythmia. Tempo's exceptionally well balanced. Look, Professor Klauson, there is still no logical reason for your being here. But meanwhile, these charts don't fib. But I'm not so smug as to think we know so much about the old cortex. Still, logically, we can't find a reason."

"But there must be a—"

"Oh, we'll find out, Professor. How do you feel now? The harmonics working all right?"

"Not quite. Dunnel, both times I have been, well, terribly afraid *before the attacks*. Some kind of intuition. My wife noticed it, too."

"You're beginning to build delusions and rationalizations. We must guard against that. You're bound to put undue emphasis on it, make it far more complex and important than it really is, because it happened at such critical moments. You deal in absolutes, Professor. Cause must equal effect."

"But it wasn't coincidence either time," insisted Klauson. "Not logically. Coincidence is too simple, too handy a gadget, Dunnel. Isn't it?"

"Maybe," said Dunnel, lighting a cigarette. "Anyway, I won't burden you with a lot of hasty probing around. The Staff says you're O.K. to leave the clinic today. Come to my office tomorrow afternoon if you feel like it. If you don't, call me up and tell me why. See you tomorrow."

A little later after the Staff had given him another thorough going-over which revealed nothing amiss, he met his wife who was waiting for him with their gyrocar on the roof-landing.

Only a third of Klauson's normal life was gone, yet he looked twice his age except for rare moments like this. He kissed Lin almost boyishly as they stood together looking over the gleaming plastic structures piercing a clear, blue sky. A soft warm summer wind blew disarmingly over Washington.

Finally Klauson said abruptly: "I'm sorry, Lin. You were right. I'll admit the obvious. Something beyond the scope of our science is blocking my progress. But what is it?"

She shook her head, her eyes brooding with concern for him, deep, dark.

"I've talked with the Science Council," she finally said in a whisper. She turned with resolution to face him. "Howard, they have agreed with me. You need a very long vacation. Our Moon House is gathering Lunar dust, if there is any. I have the Council's support now. We're going to the Moon and we're not going to think about anything that even suggests biochemistry."

"There isn't any such a thing, not on this world," said Klauson.

"Howard. We're going to raise extraterrestrial flowers."

Klauson stared, and was suddenly and violently angry.

"Flowers! You're mad!"

"But the Council's on my side, Howard. They're going to"—she paused, lips trembling—"going to accept your resignation from the Presidium."

A sick hate flooded his stomach, burst in his brain. He was stunned, impotent. He quivered silently. It was their own staff that had said there was nothing wrong with him! Yet, they were demanding that he resign! Rest on that escapist's bromide, Luna. Retreat from reality; rot in meaningless isolation.

"I'll not do it, Lin," he announced harshly. "I refuse to drop a conclusion that might mean the final step in human evolution."

He was dazed, ill, as she led him silently into the gyrocar and piloted it to their apartment. No use arguing with Lin about it. She had that ageless woman's selfish love to protect her own kind. She and the Council had combined to work against him, instead of helping him solve the cursed enigma.

As soon as they reached home, Klauson contacted the Council President, Gaudet, on the teleaudio. He argued the case, objected fiercely, begged. Gaudet was kind, logical.

"We're all so sorry, Klauson," his huge head said. "But it is quite obvious that you absolutely need a lengthy period of relaxation. Although our own staff can find no logical basis for this decision, we undoubtedly shall, and soon.

"You worked almost steadily for ten years. It is very possible that some highly specialized cellular blockage has developed that even our probers have failed to detect. A few years, raising flowers as Mrs. Klauson has suggested, something completely dissociated from your present work, is probably the answer. Then you can return to your laboratories. Meanwhile, your assistant, Larry Verrill, can continue with your research, perhaps?"

"Verrill is an excellent assistant," Klauson said, controlling himself with difficulty. "But he can never finish my work. I operate, many times, empirically; you know that. My brain alone holds the key to correlate most of the basic links of the chain."

But no amount of discussion could persuade Gaudet. It had all been definitely decided by the Council and Lin. He would retire to the Moon House by Schroeter's Canyon and raise fantastic flowers in the Moon's unique environmental conditions. He would vegetate and rot with the flowers!

"Raising flowers!" Klauson sagged, groaned helplessly, desperately.

The next afternoon in Dunnel's office with its psycho-harmonies shifting benevolently from the opaque walls, Dunnel was saying: "Fear of failure, that's one possibility; unlikely though. Doesn't check with your psycho-charts."

"There is no doubt," Klauson said. "I'm just as certain about this conclusive step as I've been about every one I've taken since I began."

"But you don't know," Dunnel pointed out, "until you've concluded and some illusive censor prevents that. Wait! Here's another possibility: maybe you're afraid of the consequences of giving humanity the ability to live forever! Think of what it would mean. Think of it consciously! I can't. It's too big. Every basic pattern completely altered. Psychology and the social sciences, particularly, would no longer apply. Humanity would become something unhuman by all present standards of evaluation. It's really an alien concept, Professor. Subconsciously, you're afraid of what it would mean!"

"I see your reasoning there, Dunnel. Frankly, I've never considered that at all. I've been so wrapped up in the thing itself."

"But let's assume that your subconscious has been working on it," insisted Dunnel. "I tell you, Professor; you go back to that laboratory of yours, right now. Get in there with all the fatal paraphernalia and just introspect for a while. Think of the whole, and go beyond the limits of your specialized course. There are so many possible consequences to a sudden transition from mortality to immortality. Think about the things that can, and will, happen. Seems to me, that might well be the motivation for the fear. And, Professor, come back and see me tomorrow."

Klauson was like the pilots who get rocket psychosis on their first Luna run, and who must immediately make another flight or lose their resistance to space-fear forever. He must go back to the laboratory. Try again.

And Dunnel's diagnosis about Klauson's possible fear of the consequences of giving humanity sudden immortality—he definitely had something there. Klauson wondered why he had never thought of it before. Like Dunnel had said, it would change every present standard of humanity. The enormity of the possible repercussion!

Klauson trembled a little with triumph. Yes, that could be the basis for the fear. A scientist must weigh the consequences of his discoveries. Would the secret of eternal life be a boon, or a catastrophe for man?

Klauson entered a public teleaudio booth and got Verrill's apartment in east Washington. Verrill's eyes seemed to have changed—they looked like those of someone else. Ridiculous. Yes, he did need a rest.

"Verrill," he said tightly, "I'm going back to the laboratory again, right now. I want you there, too."

Verrill's eyes widened, then narrowed. His mouth slipped into that sad, cynical grin.

"If you insist, Professor. And you always would, of course."

"Why—er—naturally, I will," said Klauson. "Meet me there in fifteen minutes."

The teleaudio faded, but Klauson sat there a moment. He brushed at his face wearily. So strange, the way Verrill had talked—like a stranger almost. But fifteen minutes later the vaulted height of the gleaming laboratory was very silent, and seemed, somehow, cold, as Klauson saw Verrill walking toward him. Verrill seemed to blot out the laboratory, loom extraordinarily large before him.

Klauson had unconsciously been backing away. He felt the hard cold light of the supporting column against the small of his back. He was looking fearfully, into Larry Verrill's eyes.

Into his eyes! Into incredible, swirling blackness. Into space and time and—eternity.

He was looking into incredible swirling blackness—and space and time and eternity.

And Professor H. Klauson—*knew*.

"Varro," said the thin, wavering body. "It is time for your little transmigration. The Switcher is ready. Don't think too much about what you must do. We are four-dimensional but we are still not very well adapted to the complications of the coordinate stream."

Klauson knew, yet it was far beyond his capacity to understand. He was seeing something that had happened, yet was still to happen. Fourth dimensionally, time, as he knew it, was meaningless. The man who had spoken in this strange world revealed by Verrill's alien brain, was named Grosko. The other figure, Varro, was also Verrill. Klauson knew that, but he understood very little.

Grosko's boneless fingers were manipulating the matrix coordinate console.

"I've never been convinced," muttered Varro. "It is an incomprehensible cycle, even to our fourth-dimensional minds. Where can there ever be any logical end?"

"You have already taken on some of your three-dimensional characteristics—those of Verrill, whose body you will assume control of, and merge your mentality with. Already you are beginning to think in terms of absolutes, in terms of three-dimensional logic. Forget a hypothetical end, which our fourth-dimensional consciousness knows cannot exist. You will encounter no difficulties. You will gradually adjust yourself to their concepts of the absolute; but still you will retain enough of your Varro mentality to carry out your assignment."

"But it seems so unprogressive in the Universal sense," persisted Varro. "Everything seems only a big, futile circle."

"But not for us; that is your three-dimensional absolutism creeping in already though you have not even begun merging with Verrill yet. You are beginning to make premature psychological adjustments. There are countless tangents of probability. And in the particular one that has evolved us, Professor Klauson must be prevented from completing his research. If he does, we will not evolve. But of course we have evolved, so it is inevitable that you will carry out your assignment successfully. Inevitable."

"No free agency, even in the eternal sense," mused Varro. "Everything in all dimensions of space-time is interdependent. We are aware of it, because of our fourth-dimensional minds, but those of Klauson's stage of development are not."

"That is correct," said Grosko. "They realize that everything that has happened is determined by a complex array of circumstantial causes, but they see this only in immediate, comprehensible perspective. The same is true in the Universal also, and in the time-anlim, which their three-dimensional consciousness cannot comprehend.

"Cause and effect, fourth-dimensionally, works also in what they would consider, reversal. What they see as an effect, is also cause. They tie in past, future, present, with cause and effect. Really there is no association. An effect can be in what they consider their past; and a cause can exist in their future. But you will understand after you assume possession of Verrill's consciousness."

"I hope so. It certainly seems terribly involved to me right now."

"That is a natural reaction of Verrill's mind which you are already beginning to associate yourself with. Well, Varro, you are ready for the complete alteration?"

"Naturally," said Varro. "It is on the chronosophic charts, isn't it?"

"Good-by, then," said Grosko. "Don't use the Power unless you find it absolutely necessary, then only mildly of course—"

Varro was enveloped in the radiations of the matrix. His consciousness molecules leaked slowly into the unsuspecting and narrow confines of Larry Verrill's three-dimensional consciousness as he graduated from World Tech in 2081, two years before he was to become the laboratory assistant of Professor H. Klauson.

"You—you're Varro?" Klauson managed in a hoarse whisper.

Larry Verrill nodded. A curtain had dropped over Verrill's eyes behind which those incredible, incomprehensible vistas had opened for a brief interim.

Klauson staggered. There was no basic comprehension. No two-dimensional being could imagine such a thing as *UP*.

What he termed past, present, future, to a fourth-dimensional concept would be regarded in the same way as if he, Klauson, were floating a mile in the air regarding the activities of a two-dimensional plane-man. Their only temporal sense would involve simply horizontal movement. And his three-dimensional concepts couldn't ever conceive of those of Varro's. For Varro, there was no past, present, future, as Klauson saw them.

Varro and Grosko and their world was really a future stage of man to Klauson. But Klauson and his world of 2089 was not really the past to Varro. It was only a part of the time-anlim, a term which was meaningless to Klauson. It referred to the oneness of space-time which was clearly envisioned in their fourth-dimensional minds.

"You're not—human," Klauson finally managed to say.

It sounded strange, and somewhat absurd to him after he said it.

"No," agreed Verrill or Varro. "And I might say to you, 'you're not an ape.' You think of past and future as somehow, separate. I can only tell you that it is all a kind of oneness, which we call the time-anlim. You realize now that my being here is inevitable. It isn't a matter of probability. It was never intended that you should finish this experiment, so that the present stage of humanity might live forever, forever, itself, as a word, being meaningless abstraction."

"But how can someone from the future come back through time to influence the present so that they will—"

Verrill interrupted impatiently.

"That has already been partially explained. Your three-dimensional brain can never understand it fully. Sufficient to say, Professor Klauson, that immortality, by its very nature, is impossible."

Klauson sagged despondently, futilely. He was sitting on a stool looking up. There was no impulse to escape, or to attempt to avoid what was too obviously his end.

"Why?" he asked, listlessly. "Why is immortality impossible?"

"Put it this way, Professor." Klauson winced; the voice sounded so like the harmless, youthful and rather naive Larry Verrill. "Immortality means the cessation of man's association with the process of entropy. Your developing makes another integral part of the entropic process possible. You call it evolution."

He paused, then continued. "You regard us as human. You have other labels, mutants, homo-superiors, or even supermen. But we only develop in this process called by you, evolution. Can't you see the paradox of immortality? It would be feasible if immortality was some part of the evolving process, but it isn't. It might be in some other line of probability, but not this particular one. Look into what you call the past, Professor."

Verrill's eyes were narrow, inscrutable.

"If the ape had suddenly developed immortality, you wouldn't have evolved. Thinking man could never have evolved from an immortal and therefore stagnant race of apes. Just as mortal man came from apes, so homo-superior evolves from mortal man. Paradoxically, there can be no immortality, if the true racial chain is to survive."

Klauson sat stiffly. Well, Dunnel had gotten close to the correct solution though he could never dream of the truth. There had been a deeply buried subconscious fear of the results of immortality. It would have destroyed the—well, what he called 'man's future.' But there was one thing that might be explained.

"Why have you allowed me to advance as far as I have in my research?"

Verrill smiled sadly. "Your whole concept is based on false logic," he said. "But I can't explain. There isn't a question of *allowing* you. You see, you had to develop this far with your experimentation. Your work involving cosmic ray treatment of genes resulted in certain germ plasm alteration in certain individuals. This will bring about our fourth-dimensional emergence in what you call 'later,' as mutants."

"Then," said Klauson faintly, "I'm also responsible for you."

The young man nodded. "You would term it that. But it's all an integral whole. You deal in cause and effect. But the closest you can get to our logic is to hyphenate it endlessly, cause-effect-cause-effect-cause-effect-cause-effect-cause-effect-cause-effect, without end."

There was a heavy silence. Then Verrill said, not unkindly, "I had better take care of you now, Professor. Your mind will have to bear far too much strain. Your reasoning processes will demand an explanation, which for your three-dim consciousness, is impossible. You will develop a psychosis unless I alter your mind sufficiently."

"What are you going to do?" whispered Klauson, his mouth dry.

"By suggestion, I'll alter your basic behavior and motivation patterns. You will retain most of your present mental characteristics. Amnesia followed by new and fundamentally different lines of activity."

Klauson started to run away, but he found himself sucked into a whirling maelstrom of senseless, unrelated chaos. He reeled dizzily. He felt himself falling....

He saw his laboratory assistant, Larry Verrill, standing above him, saying with nervous concern, "Professor, you've fainted again. You all right now?"

Klauson felt a queer shocking sensation, an intangible impulse, rather painful.

"No, Larry," he replied. "It's over with me now. I really don't think I could have succeeded in achieving immortality for mankind anyway. There's a flaw in the chain of development, somewhere. And the whole procedure is so complex we could never go over it and find the error. Goodnight, Larry. I'm going home."

He didn't wait for his gyrocar to reach his apartment to tell Lin the startling developments. He contacted her by teleaudio.

"I've changed my mind, Lin dear. I've decided to accept your and the Council's advice. Get together everything we'll want to take to Moon House with us. And, by the way, get all the microfilm you can find on botany and extraterrestrial horticulture. I wonder what has been the matter with me all my life?"

Her face shone with a lovely pink flush of happiness as it faded from the small screen.

Klauson relaxed as the gyrocar sped toward his apartment. His eyes closed, his day-dream was one of glorious technicolor, overflowing with mental reproductions of the magnificent flowers he and Lin would grow in the quiet comfort of the Lunarian valleys.

Milton Keynes UK
Ingram Content Group UK Ltd.
UKHW041820151124
451262UK00005B/706